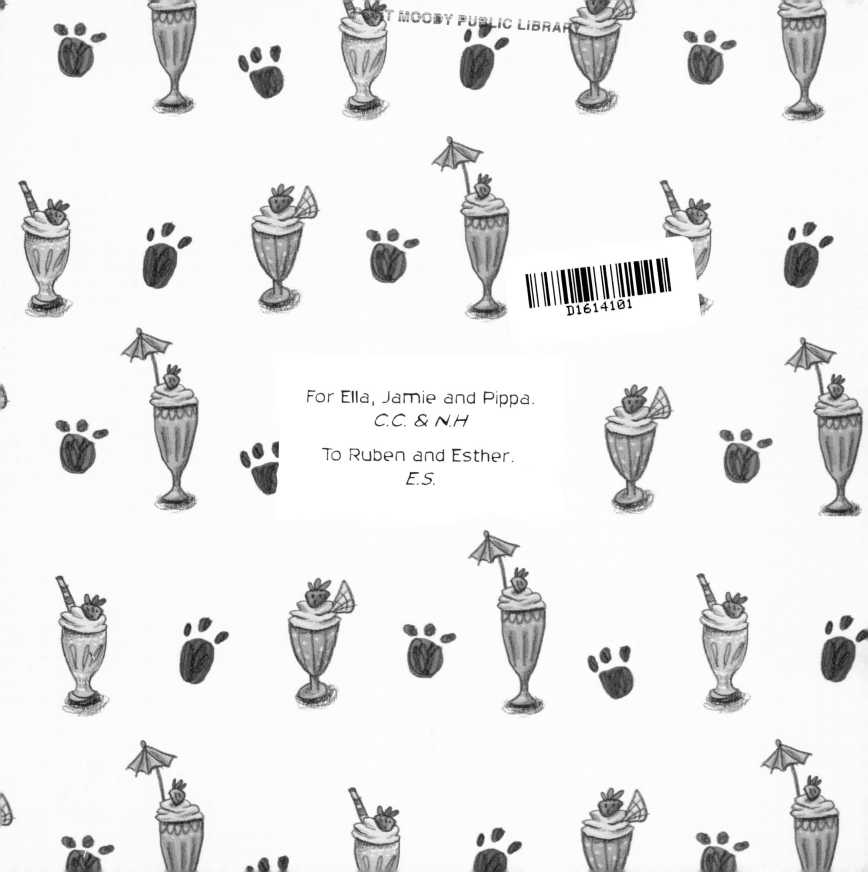

MOODY PUBLIC LIBRARY

D1614101

For Ella, Jamie and Pippa.
C.C. & N.H

To Ruben and Esther.
E.S.

First published in 2017
by Jessica Kingsley Publishers
73 Collier Street
London N1 9BE, UK
and
400 Market Street, Suite 400
Philadelphia, PA 19106, USA

www.jkp.com

Copyright © Chris Calland and Nicky Hutchinson 2017
Illustrations copyright © Emmi Smid 2017

All rights reserved. No part of this publication may
be reproduced in any material form (including
photocopying, storing in any medium by electronic
means or transmitting) without the written permission
of the copyright owner except in accordance with
the provisions of the law or under terms of a licence
issued in the UK by the Copyright Licensing Agency
Ltd. www.cla.co.uk or in overseas territories by the
relevant reproduction rights organisation, for details
see www.ifrro.org. Applications for the copyright
owner's written permission to reproduce any part of
this publication should be addressed to the publisher.

Warning: The doing of an unauthorised act in
relation to a copyright work may result in both a
civil claim for damages and criminal prosecution.

Library of Congress Cataloging in Publication Data
A CIP catalog record for this book is
available from the Library of Congress

British Library Cataloguing in Publication Data
A CIP catalogue record for this book is
available from the British Library

ISBN 978 1 78592 233 6
eISBN 978 1 78450 514 1

Printed and bound in China

of related interest

Banish Your Body Image Thief
A Cognitive Behavioural Therapy Workbook on
Building Positive Body Image for Young People
Kate Collins-Donnelly
ISBN 978 1 84905 463 8
eISBN 978 0 85700 842 8
Gremlin and Thief CBT Workbooks series

Your Body is Awesome
Body Respect for Children
Sigrun Danielsdottir
Illustrated by Bjork Bjarkdottir
ISBN 978 1 84819 228 7
eISBN 978 0 85701 178 7

Positive Body Image for Kids
A Strengths-Based Curriculum for Children Aged 7–11
Ruth MacConville
ISBN 978 1 84905 539 0
eISBN 978 1 78450 047 4

Minnie & Max are OK!

Chris Calland and
Nicky Hutchinson

Illustrated by Emmi Smid

Jessica Kingsley Publishers
London and Philadelphia

This is Minnie playing with her dog Max. Grandma often looks after them and she says they never sit still!

When Minnie gets picked up from school by Max and Grandma, three things usually happen:

Max jumps up at Minnie. Minnie shouts "Relax Max!" then she gives him a friendly scratch just behind his ears.

Then, on the way home, Minnie likes to skip, hop or walk sideways, asking Grandma all kinds of questions.

Max quite often asks himself things too.

But today was different. Minnie walked along quietly without asking anything at all. And Max just asked himself one question: "Why didn't Minnie shout 'Relax Max!' and make a fuss of me at the school gate?"

"You seem a bit down in the dumps, Minnie," said Grandma. "Is there something the matter?"

"Yes," Minnie whispered. She was feeling fed up. School had not gone at all well today. At playtime two girls wouldn't let her play with them. They'd laughed at her, saying, "You look silly!" She had thought about it all day.

Grandma took Minnie's hand and gave it a squeeze. "I thought we could stop at the park for a little while on our way home. How would you like that?" Minnie smiled and nodded her head. "Yes please!" she replied. "Max would like that too!" Max wagged his tail.

On their way to the park they passed the local shops. Minnie noticed her reflection in a window. She saw a small girl with a mass of brown curly hair. She was wearing her school clothes and a pair of worn out black shoes.

Fruit & Veg

Open

Organic Happy Eggs

Pota

Max stared at his own reflection. He saw short legs and scruffy fur, the colour of biscuits.

Minnie frowned and scuffed her shoes as she walked along. "I'd like to be tall like Samir," she thought to herself. "If only I had long straight hair like Ella..." "I wish I looked different."

Max raised his nose in the air and tried to walk like a poodle. Minnie walked on tiptoes to be taller. She scraped her hair down to flatten it against her head.

"What are you two up to?" laughed Grandma, as Minnie and Max both walked through the park gates in a most peculiar way.

"Why don't we go and get a drink first?"
Grandma suggested. Minnie was always
thirsty after school and the park café
served brilliant milkshakes. Minnie and
Max led the way there, up the slope and
past the fountain.

If only I had long legs so that I could run like that!

In the café Minnie chose a banana and strawberry milkshake, which had a real strawberry perched on the top. Grandma ordered a cup of tea and Max had a bowl of fresh water.

"I don't really like how I look," Minnie said in a small voice as they sat down with their drinks. "I wish I looked more like my friends."

I'd like a smart collar like that one!

"Well I wouldn't change anything about you, I love you just exactly the way you are!" exclaimed Grandma. "I think it's wonderful that we all look so different. People come in all sorts of shapes, sizes and colours," she said. "Just look around us."

There were lots of children in the park. They were tall, short, little and large. They had dark skin, light skin, curly hair and straight hair. There were children with glasses, some with freckles and some were wearing headscarves. Everyone really does look different, thought Minnie.

...8, 9, 10!

Max stared at all the dogs in the park. There were so many types! Black, white, sandy-coloured, spotty, scary, friendly, short, long-tailed, shaggy, fierce, tiny and enormous.

Grandma smiled at Minnie and Max.
"Imagine how boring it would be if
we all looked the same!" she said.

Looking round at all the children, Minnie spotted Samir and Ella from her school. "Why don't you go and join them?" suggested Grandma. Minnie and Max ran over to be with her friends.

They made up some new games to play. Ella was the fastest at "Can't Catch Me," and Minnie told Samir he had the fiercest growl when they played "Bears in the Forest."

Wow, that dog can really jump!

But "Max in the Middle" was definitely the game Max enjoyed the most!

Minnie thought of a new game, which she called "Monkey Trees." "We need to be monkeys and climb up here," she explained, pulling herself up on the climbing frame. "You always think of really good games, Minnie," said Samir, as he and Ella scrambled up beside her.

OOOOH OOH AH AH

Minnie held on tight and swung backwards to hang by her legs. Samir and Ella watched carefully, then copied her.

When they were all hanging upside down they giggled and made loud monkey noises together.

"It must be brilliant to be a monkey," Minnie thought, "they can swing by their tails and climb all day."

Grandma was watching from the café and called out, "Come on, you noisy monkeys, it's time to go now!"

Minnie jumped down from the climbing frame and shouted goodbye to her friends.

In the café, Grandma got up to pay for the drinks. As she counted the money she pointed out the photograph of Minnie's dad that she kept tucked in a little window inside her purse.

"Look at this picture of your dad when he was little, Minnie," she said. "He had the same mop of curls as you. And he was always on the go – it must be where you get your energy from!"

Minnie peered at the picture and then looked carefully
at Grandma's face and grinned.

"I've got exactly the same colour eyes as you too, haven't I Grandma?"

Minnie bent down to give Max a pat and she rubbed the soft, scruffy fur just under his chin. She was smiling.

"I look just like my dad and my grandma," she told him.

As they
walked home
from the park,
Minnie skipped along
the pavement sideways
and asked Grandma some
important questions.

"Did you see us playing
monkey trees?"

"Do you think monkeys like
strawberries as well as bananas?"

"Isn't Max brilliant at catching?"

"Yes, he certainly is a talented dog,"
agreed Grandma. "And what a good
climber you are Minnie!"

As they turned the corner into their street, Minnie began singing her favourite song and Max joined in straight away.

"Oh noooo," moaned Grandma.

Minnie laughed and bent down to give Max a scratch behind his ears. "I really liked being a monkey," she whispered to him,

"but it's even better being me!"

Suggested questions to help children explore the topic further

Teasing

- What could you do or say if someone was unkind to you or teased you? Who could help you?

- If you saw Minnie looking unhappy in the playground what would you do or say to her?

What we look like

- What do you see when you look in the mirror? How would you describe yourself?

- What do you like about how you look?

- Does anyone look perfect?

Who we look like[1]

- Do people ever say you look like someone in your family?

- Why do you think Minnie is pleased to look like her dad and grandma?

- Max wishes he looked like other dogs. Do you think Minnie would like him to look different?

---

1   Some children who are adopted or in care may not know their birth family, although many will have seen photos. Discussing the looks they inherited from their birth parents can be helpful in developing their sense of identity.

Diversity

- What would it be like if everyone looked the same? How would people know you? How would you know your friends and family?

- If everyone looked exactly the same, do you think they would all be identical on the inside?

- Would you like it if everyone looked the same?

- Think about all the people and dogs in the park. Can you list all the ways that they look different?

What our bodies can do

- Our bodies are amazing and can do all sorts of fantastic things. Can you think of all the things Minnie and Max can do with their bodies?

- What can you do with your body? (Perhaps you could run a talent show or obstacle course to celebrate what you can do!)

Celebrating our skills

- What is Minnie good at doing?

- What are Max's skills?

- Everyone has different skills and strengths. What are you good at? What about your friends?

- Is there anyone who is good at everything?!

At the end of the book, how do you think Minnie and Max feel about themselves? Why?

Chris and Nicky are teachers and specialist education consultants with over 25 years' experience of working in children's behaviour and mental health. After many years as advisers for Bristol local authority they founded their own consultancy, "Not Just Behaviour," and they work internationally with parents, schools and health professionals to develop children's self-esteem and body confidence. They co-authored the award-winning book, *Body Image in the Primary School* (David Fulton, 2011).

Chris and Nicky advise the government on how to promote a healthy body image in boys and girls and believe it is vital to begin this work when children are young.

They are both parents and understand the joys and challenges of raising a family in the 21st century. For more information about Chris, Nicky and their work, please visit www.notjustbehaviour.co.uk.

Emmi was born in the Netherlands. She finished both her Bachelor in Fine Art and her Masters in Sequential Design/ Illustration in the UK. Emmi writes and illustrates picture books that highlight social taboos and current global topics. She previously published *Luna's Red Hat* with Jessica Kingsley Publishers (2015). For more information about Emmi or her work, please visit www.emmismid.nl.